Annie and Snowball and the Pink Surprise

The Fourth Book of Their Adventures

Cynthia Rylant
Illustrated by Suçie Stevenson

READY-TO-READ

ALADDIN

New York   London   Toronto   Sydney

To two little bunnies, Snowball and Lily
—C. R.

For Pop and Josie
—S. S.

ALADDIN
An imprint of Simon & Schuster Children's Publishing Division
1230 Avenue of the Americas, New York, NY 10020
First Aladdin paperback edition February 2010
Text copyright © 2008 by Cynthia Rylant
Illustrations copyright © 2008 by Suçie Stevenson
ALADDIN is a trademark of Simon & Schuster, Inc.,
and related logo is a registered trademark of Simon & Schuster, Inc.
READY-TO-READ is a registered trademark of Simon & Schuster, Inc.
Also available in a Simon & Schuster Books for Young Readers hardcover edition.
For information about special discounts for bulk purchases, please contact Simon &
Schuster Special Sales at 1-866-506-1949 or business@simonandschuster.com.
The Simon & Schuster Speakers Bureau can bring authors to your live event. For more
information or to book an event contact the Simon & Schuster Speakers Bureau at
1-866-248-3049 or visit our website at www.simonspeakers.com.
Designed by Tom Daly
The text of this book was set in Goudy Old Style.
The illustrations for this book were rendered in pen-and-ink and watercolor.
Manufactured in the United States of America
0412 LAK
4 6 8 10 9 7 5
The Library of Congress has cataloged the hardcover edition as follows:
Rylant, Cynthia.
Annie and Snowball and the pink surprise/Cynthia Rylant;
Illustrated by Suçie Stevenson—1st ed.
p. cm.
Summary: After noticing that a visiting hummingbird likes her pink petunias,
Annie and her rabbit, Snowball, accompanied by Henry and his dog, Mudge,
fill the garden with pink objects to attract more hummingbirds.
ISBN 978-1-4169-0941-5 (hc)
[1. Hummingbirds—Fiction. 2. Gardens—Fiction. 3. Pets—Fiction.]
I. Stevenson, Suçie, ill. II. Title.
PZ7.R982 Ano 2008
[E]—dc22
2007020483
ISBN 978-1-4169-1462-4 (pbk)

Contents

Annie's Garden

Annie and her bunny, Snowball,
liked to grow flowers in
Annie's backyard.

5

Annie had petunias and
lilies and roses and four o'clocks.
(Four o'clocks were her favorites.)

When Annie's cousin Henry
(who lived next door) would come over
with his big dog, Mudge,
sometimes they all would sit in
Annie's garden.

"Be careful, Mudge," Annie would say.
"Don't squash the four o'clocks."
Mudge was careful.
He didn't squash the four o'clocks.
But he did drool on
a few lilies.

Snowball just liked to
hide in the roses.

"I see you, Snowball!"
Henry would call.
Snowball would just
wiggle her nose.

9

A Visitor!

One day when Annie and Henry
were in the garden, they saw
the most wonderful sight:
a hummingbird!

A hummingbird was drinking
from a petunia!
"Oh!" said Annie.
"Wow!" said Henry. "I've never seen
a hummingbird!"

11

Mudge and Snowball
didn't really care.
They were napping.

But Annie and Henry
were so excited.

And they wondered how they could
get more hummingbirds
to come to Annie's garden.
They started thinking.

"More petunias?" asked Henry.
"I've spent my whole allowance
already," said Annie.
"I can't buy any more petunias."

"Hmmm," said Henry. "Well, we
will just have to advertise."
"Advertise?" asked Annie.
"Sure," said Henry. "We have to let
more hummingbirds know
that you're here. And that you
have petunias."

"How do we let them know?"
asked Annie, picking up Snowball
and rubbing her ears.

"Let's ask my dad," said Henry.
"He says he knows *everything*."
Annie smiled.

They found Henry's dad in his garage.

He was making a bookcase.

Or trying to.

18

It was a little crooked.

"It's a little crooked, Dad,"
Henry said.

"Hmmm," said Henry's dad.

He stepped back.
"Well, I'll just have to buy only
books that lean to the right," he said.
Annie laughed.
Henry's dad was so silly.

"Dad, we need to attract
hummingbirds," said Henry.
"Do you know how?"
"Hmmm," said Henry's dad.

"How about petunias?"
"I have petunias," said Annie,
"but only one hummingbird."
"Hmmm," said Henry's dad again.

He thought for a minute while
Snowball crawled on his head
and Mudge sat on his foot.

"Maybe colors," he finally said.
"Maybe more
colors in the garden."

"What color are your petunias?"
he asked Annie.
"Pink," said Annie.
"Then pink it is," said Henry's dad.
"Put more pink in the garden and
see what happens."

He looked again at his bookcase.
"Maybe I'll buy books that lean
to the right and we'll move to a house
that leans to the left," he said.
Henry and Annie just smiled.

Very Pink

"Pink stuff," said Henry as they
walked back to Annie's house.
"We need pink stuff."

He looked at Annie.

"You should have plenty of pink stuff,"
he said. "You're nothing *but* pink!"

"I know," said Annie.

"Let's check my room!"

They went to Annie's room.

Pink everywhere!

Henry picked up a small chair.

"Pink!" he said.

He picked up a large ball.

"Pink again!"

Henry and Annie loaded up
ten very pink things and
took them to Annie's garden.

30

They set them in strange high places
for hummingbirds to see.

"I sure hope this works," said Annie.

"Me too," said Henry.

"Because if it doesn't,
I'm going to feel pretty silly."

Annie looked at Henry holding
a pink umbrella.
"You look pretty silly now," she said.
And she giggled and giggled.

Come and See!

It took four days.
Annie and Snowball sat in the
garden every morning, hoping for
hummingbirds.

Nothing on the first day.
Nothing on the second day.
One on the third day.
And *eight* on the fourth day!
Eight hummingbirds!

Annie ran over to get Henry.
"Come and see!" she said.
Henry and Mudge hurried
to Annie's garden.
And there they saw eight beautiful,
tiny hummingbirds
drinking from Annie's petunias.

"They like pink," said Annie.
"Maybe they just like
umbrellas," Henry said.

A hummingbird suddenly
darted over.
It hovered above Mudge's head.
"Or maybe they just
like *Mudge*," said Annie.
"Well, who wouldn't?" asked Henry.

Then Annie and Snowball and
Henry and Mudge spent
the whole morning
watching their wonderful birds.